For you are fearfully and wonderfully made...

PSALMS 139

On the Night You Were Born

Nancy Tillman

FEIWEL AND FRIENDS

New York

On the night you were born,
the moon smiled with such wonder
that the stars peeked in to see you
and the night wind whispered,
"Life will never be the same."

Because there had never been anyone like you...
ever in the world.

So enchanted with you were the wind and the rain
that they whispered the sound of your wonderful name.

The sound of your  name is a magical one.
Let's say it out loud before we go on.

You are the one and only ever you...

It sailed through the farmland
high on the breeze...

Who in the world is exactly like you
Who   Who   Who

Over the ocean...

you are wonderful

You are a miracle

And through the trees...

Until everyone heard it
and everyone knew
of the one and only ever you.

Not once had there been such eyes,
such a nose,
such silly, wiggly, wonderful toes.

In fact, I think I'll count to three
so you can wiggle your toes for me.

When the polar bears heard,
they danced until dawn.

From faraway places,
the geese flew home.

The moon stayed up until morning next day.

And none of the ladybugs flew away.

So whenever you doubt just how special you are
and you wonder who loves you, how much and how far,
listen for geese honking high in the sky.
(They're singing a song to remember you by.)

Or notice the bears asleep at the zoo.
(It's because they've been dancing all night for you!)

Or drift off to sleep to the sound of the wind.
(Listen closely...it's whispering your name again!)

If the moon stays up until morning one day,
or a ladybug lands and decides to stay,
or a little bird sits at your window awhile,
it's because they're all hoping to see you smile...

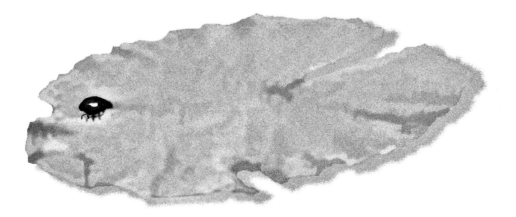

For never before in story or rhyme
(not even once upon a time)
has the world ever known a you, my friend,
and it never will, not ever again...

Heaven blew every trumpet
and played every horn
on the wonderful, marvelous
night you were born.

wonderful... marvelous... you...

To Tucker and Tess, who are fearfully and wonderfully made.

A Feiwel and Friends Book
An Imprint of Macmillan

On the Night You Were Born. Copyright © 2005 by Nancy Tillman. All rights reserved. Printed in China. No part of this book may be used or reproduced in any manner whatsoever without written permission except in the case of brief quotations embodied in critical articles or reviews. For information, address Feiwel and Friends, 175 Fifth Avenue, New York, N.Y. 10010.

Library of Congress Cataloging-in-Publication Data available

ISBN-13: 978-0-312-34606-5
ISBN-10: 0-312-34606-9

Feiwel and Friends logo designed by Filomena Tuosto
First published in the United States by Darling Press LLC

20 19 18 17 16 15 14 13 12
www.feiwelandfriends.com

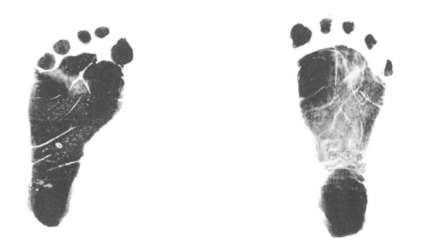

You are loved.